My Spiritual Awakening

My Spiritual Awakening

THE TRUTH NO LONGER HURTS

By: Valencia Lee

Illustrated By: Asia Penelton

Valencia Lee Publishing Company

Valencia Lee Publishing Company LLC

Contents

To my son, Legend, for making me a better person

Part 1

Where It All Began

I was born and raised in Oak Cliff, Texas. A sizable urban neighborhood in Dallas, Texas, where the residents felt their hood was its own city. We took pride in our savage, roguish behavior, and our attitudes were ruthless. Besides, it is the city where President John F. Kennedy was assassinated. That's why we call it the Dirty Dirty D!

It was me, my mama, and my little brother, Mondre'. We didn't live in the projects but it was the next best thing. Our apartments had two swimming pools. Mondre' and I had a bad reputation in Oak Cliff. We were always in trouble. For whatever reason, whenever something went down, people always accused us of having some kind of involvement. For example, when the apartments caught on fire, cars were stolen, or sneaking into people's houses at night; it always came back to one of us. It didn't help that Mondre' and one of his friends were caught red handed urinating on someone's car while standing on our third-floor balcony.

The children in our hood, including myself, had a reputation of "rocking" people in the pool. If someone in my crew disliked you or had a problem with you and we saw you at the pool, you were getting rocked! Everyone would congregate around the pool or get out of the pool when we saw you. We would wait for you to get into the pool and strongly encouraged you to get into the deep water, at least 8 feet. When you jumped in, or we threw you in, we would all jump in the pool together right afterward. We'd developed a technique where you ball up your body in a cannonball style, but it will create more of a splash and more giant waves if you land on your lower back and upper buttocks. So, when you came above water, the waves surrounding you covered you entirely, uncontrollably. It caused you to panic in emerging waters, which eventually led to many problems in the future, as you can imagine.

At the time, I didn't consider myself a bully or a dominant person. Still, I wasn't going to let anyone punk me either. On my first day of elementary school, this boy in my class tried to skip me in line. There was no way anyone else was going to be in the front of the line except for me. I wasn't having it, so I hit him in the back of his head with my backpack. He hit me back, and before you knew it, we were wrestling on the floor. I was suspended for fighting.

I did whatever I wanted to in the hood. My daddy was never around because he was a crack addict. I don't know where my mama was or what she was doing. When I wasn't in school or defending Mondre', I spent most of my time at Thurgood Marshall Recreation Center playing basketball. Or in a quiet place writing about everything going on in my life. Violence was at an all-time high and all around me. When I was 5 years old, Mondre' shot me with a .22 caliber gun. As the gun went off, the bullet-headed directly between my eyes, towards the middle of my forehead.

I learned at an early age that I had special protection. I didn't know what to call it, but angels were protecting me because the bullet grazed my left ear and shattered the window behind me. My life was no walk in the park but more like walking up a mountain during an avalanche. You could be at the rec center hooping with someone one day, and a couple of hours later, find out they just murdered someone or were just killed. Every day was a surprise!

After multiple suspensions for fighting, I found out I was smart. I was an honor roll student, enrolled in the gifted and talented program, and our girls' basketball team won the district championship in elementary. Yet, I stayed in the principal's office and had to report to the guidance counselor three times a week. There were a lot of things going on at my home, and I didn't know how to talk about it. I thought domestic violence was normal. By middle school, my relationship with my mama had gotten so bad, we just couldn't live together. I was back and forth between my granny and God mama's house.

In my freshman year of high school, I decided I didn't want to go to school anymore. I was a truant, and the Dallas Independent School District reported my mama to the county. The judge put out a warrant for her arrest. A couple of days later, we went to the county court before the judge, and he announced that I'd missed 65 out of 72 days of school. He wanted an explanation, and of course, I didn't have one, except I just didn't feel like going. Out of nowhere, my mama had a loud, emotional outburst. She told the judge she didn't know what to do with me anymore, and she didn't want to go to jail. The judge called me into his chambers and talked with me about my behavior. An hour later, he let us go with a slap on the wrist and made me and mama go to a court-mandated class.

When my mama and I left the courthouse, she was still emotional and told me that I could drop out of high school if I wanted to. She made it very clear that she wasn't going to jail because I didn't want to go to school. I agreed with her. So, my mama told me we would come back to the courthouse tomorrow morning to sign the paperwork for me to drop out of school. When I got back to my apartment complex, I bragged and told everyone I didn't have to go to school anymore.

Later that night, my granny found out about me and my mama's plan. I thought it was the end of the world. My granny and papa unexpectedly showed up at our home, and my papa was at the front door telling me to pack my things. It was strange because my grandparents didn't drive at night or to our apartments in the hood. I packed my things and left with my papa. When I got into the car, my granny told me I was going to school, and dropping out was not an option!

After I moved in with my grandparents, I transferred from Kimball High school to Carter High School. I joined the basketball team, National Honor Society, and Student Council. I was on the honor roll and enrolled in advanced placement classes. I was seventeen when I graduated from high school with honors and managed to graduate in the Top 10% of my class. I was even more shocked when I received an academic scholarship to Texas A&M University in College Station. My initial decision was to join the United States Marines. I regularly trained for the physical exam and studied with my mentor daily for the ASVAB exam. I thought I was going in at a great time because the United States had just entered war with Iraq and Afghanistan. I wanted to travel, and I knew I wouldn't get bored. But my granny was firmly against my decision and persuaded me to accept the scholarship. So, I did. I really didn't care. I just wanted to get away from Dallas.

Self Destruction

College was difficult, and adapting to the small, racist college town was hell! The residents and students there made it an agenda to make us suffer. They did not want Blacks in their town and that year the Black population doubled because Texas A&M University had to recruit more Blacks to receive federal funding.

The same year, the university made national news because some white students posted a racist video online portraying themselves to be Black. I started to regret my decision to attend there, but my only other choice was to go back to Oak Cliff. So, I turned to drugs instead. Pills, weed, cough syrup, and alcohol became my family and friends.

During college, I had made every possible wrong decision one could make. However, I still managed to graduate with my bachelor's degree. God still had a plan for me! When I walked across the stage, I felt untouchable. Like I had taken over the world. Only to realize life had gotten real after graduation, and I was not prepared at all.

After college, I had been offered several high-paying jobs and accepted a position at a political firm in Dallas, Texas. For the first time, I was excited to go back home. The day my lease was up, and I was moving out of my apartment, my mama informed me that she was having relationship problems, and it was not a suitable time for me to move back. I called around to other relatives and asked if I could temporarily live with them. I was willing to get a part-time job at Mcdonald's to get my own place as soon as possible. But everyone said no. There I was with a degree from Texas A&M University, homeless, and nowhere to go.

Later that night, I had all of my things packed on the back of my friend's truck. I was moving to Houston, Texas, with my best friend, Sharda. She was in her last year of undergraduate at Prairie View A&M University. Every morning we woke up, took multiple shots of Patron, smoked several blunts, and based on our plans for the day on which and how many pills we popped. Months went by, and I became angrier and angrier at the condition of my life. My drug addiction had gotten worse, and I'd self-destructed.

My friendship with Sharda began to depreciate, and she stopped coming home and started hanging out with other people. I continued to live there. Me and her roommate, Daniel, started hanging out when he was not working. This was too much for his girlfriend though. She accused me of sleeping with Daniel. A few days later, she and three of her friends came over to attack me. I'm still unsure exactly what happened. But one of the girls got injured badly, so they took her to the hospital and made a police report against me. Law enforcers came to the townhouse to get my side of the story. I was forced to move out, and I was homeless again.

I moved back to College Station with my boyfriend, Poe. He had recently gotten an apartment and had been bugging me to live with him. I did not have anywhere else to go, so I agreed. Within weeks I was working at Best Buy, Blockbuster, and Papa John's. I was exhausted, depressed, and miserable. I was 24 years old with a bachelor's degree making $10 an hour. I did the only logical thing I knew to do when life got rough. I started going back to church. I went to Sunday School, regular Church service, Bible Study, or any other service they were having when I was not working. The church became my home, and I enjoyed being there. It took me a while but eventually, I joined and became a member.

One Sunday, I took off all my jobs to go to Sunday school, church service, and Pastor's and wife's anniversary dinner. I dreaded the next day because I had to work all three jobs, and my day began at 5:00 am and did not end till midnight. Then I had to get back up and do it all over again the following day. After a couple of days, I was over it!

That morning, Poe came and picked me up from work at 2:00 am. I had to be back at work at 6:00 am. When I arrived home, all I wanted to do was shower and go to sleep. But Poe's brothers, cousins, and friends were there in our one-bedroom apartment. I flipped on everyone when I heard the music, loud chatter, and clouds of smoke everyone was indulging in without me, that I had not had all day. I went to the kitchen, grabbed the knife, then went into the bathroom to grab the gun. I yelled and told everyone to get out of my house!

People began to scatter as I angrily screamed. I walked outside with the weapons in my hand. The neighbor upstairs timidly walked past me as the commotion was going on. Finally, everyone left. Poe apologized for being inconsiderate and ran me a hot bubble bath. While I was bathing, he rolled me two blunts. We smoked, and he gave me a full body massage. He gently kissed me on my neck then slowly down my back. Suddenly, there were three loud, obnoxious knocks at the front door. I instantly jumped up and looked at Poe in fear. Then, we heard the loud knocks again. He looked at me and said, "That's the police!"

Poe got up and started hiding the large amount of marijuana we had in the apartment. I did not want to open the door. I looked for an exit, but there was only one way out and the police had the apartment surrounded. We could see their flashlights through the windows. They knocked again, but this time warning us. They were knocking the door down in 3 ... 2 ... 1. I opened the door just as he was about to knock it down. The Special Weapons and Tactics team held their massive automatic weapons towards me and told me to put my hands up.

The next day I woke up in jail and vaguely remembered what happened. When I spoke to the judge, she informed me I was being charged with Aggravated Assault with a Deadly Weapon and resisting arrest. Apparently, it took four officers to handcuff me. I was only 5' 7" and weighed 130 pounds. I had let my anger consume and control me at its best. It had not been a year since I had graduated from college, and now I was facing felony charges.

I found out quickly that I was not made for jail. I was only allowed one roll of toilet paper per day. Obviously, that was not enough for me because I was trading my meals for toilet paper. It did not matter to me anyway. The food was terrible!

I called my daddy, who was the only person I knew would understand my foolish actions. He was adamant about helping me get out. I called him every chance I got wondering when I was bailing out. But he informed me that it was Labor Day weekend, and the banks were closed, so I was stuck in jail for 3 days.

Part 2

The Reflection of Myself

When I got out of jail, I heard God's voice more clearly than I had ever heard while walking to the church. But by then, I did not want to hear it anymore. I just wanted to speak with the Pastor and let him know that God had failed me again. I was still living with Poe and fired from all my jobs because I went to jail. No call. No show. Although I had a case pending, I needed to get out of College Station.

A month later, I moved to East Texas with my daddy and grandma, his mama. This was the first time I'd lived with my daddy as an adult. I enjoyed spending time with my grandma. While I was growing up, I had heard lots of stories from family members about my daddy. Still, I often overlooked them because I loved my daddy. I was his only child. He had broken many promises to me over the years. But during this time, I got to see him for who he indeed was.

My case was pending in College Station for a year before

I made a plea. I refused to have a felony on my record, so my court date kept getting pushed back as my lawyer, Ciara Dawkins, negotiated with the District Attorney. I was blessed to have a close friend with a law degree. I traveled back and forth from Mount Pleasant, Texas, to College Station on the Greyhound bus every three weeks for court. I mostly lived in Mount Pleasant with my daddy and grandma. I would see Poe when I had court.

My daddy and grandma made sure I had everything I needed, but I still felt useless because I could not provide for myself. I got a job at a car lot, repossessing cars, and a part-time job at McDonald's. My dad and I had the best relationship I could ever imagine. We went fishing as often as possible, played dominoes, and watched the news for comedy. Occasionally, we would smoke a joint. But this did not last long, though. My daddy's actions started to disgust me, and I could not stand to look at him. He knew it too! I kept my distance, stayed in my room, and wrote when I had some free time.

My grandma often went to the casino on the weekends with her sisters and would leave me her car with restrictions not to let my dad drive her car. One Friday night, she and her four sisters headed out, and she left the keys behind for me after making me repeat the rules to her multiple times. After she left, I met up with some co-workers for dinner and drinks at the last minute and made it back home around 11:00 pm. I prepared for work the following day and showered before getting into bed.

Around 3:00 am, my cell phone started ringing and vibrating. It was my dad, so I declined the call and turned off my phone. Then he called the landline phone. I picked it up and instantly hung up the phone when I heard his voice. He called again. Finally, I answered. He asked me to come to pick him up. We were in a small town, and I was not familiar with where he was. From the tone of his voice, he was under the influence of drugs. I told him, "No! I had to go to work in the morning, did not have time for his games, and hung up the phone. He called again. I took the phone off the hook so it would not ring anymore.

I fell back asleep, and about thirty minutes later, I was awakened by a door slamming. I jumped up out of my sleep. I stayed there waiting to hear another sound. Before I knew it, my daddy was busting into my grandma's room, yelling about him having to walk thirty minutes in the middle of the night to get home. He continued yelling. You could tell by the slur in his words and how he behaved that he was higher than the sky. I was scared and afraid for my life. I could tell by the look in my dad's eye that he was willing to do anything at that moment to prove his point, whether he was right or wrong. I reached behind my grandma's bed for her shotgun. He continued screaming and began approaching me. I pointed the rifle at him and cocked it back. I told him, "You have fucked over everyone in this family, and they have let you live. I am your seed. The Seed of Chucky. If you come one step closer to me, you are about to meet the creator himself!"

I do not know if it was the tone in my voice. Or the look in my eyes. Or the fact my dad realized I was telling the truth, but he left the room. I packed up my things and went to a motel room for the rest of the morning until I had to go to work. The next morning, I called Ciara and begged her to hurry and make a plea.

A few more months went by, Ciara was able to get my felony reduced to a misdemeanor, and the resisting arrest charges dropped. But there was a catch! I had to do one-year probation and thirty days in jail. The thought of me having to go back to jail made me lose my mind, but I was ready to get this behind me. Luckily, some paperwork got messed up, and I only ended up doing 3 nights during the weekend. Now, trying not to do drugs while on probation was my biggest challenge!

I moved back to Houston, Texas, with my little brother, Mondre'. He was a senior at the University of Houston and had a townhouse on the southside. I had gotten a job selling vacuum cleaners, and after a month of working, finally, I got myself a car. I loved being in Houston. Most of my college friends lived there, while some of my closest friends from Dallas, including Ciara, moved there too. It felt like home.

Pregnant

When I got my car, I would drive to College Station to see Poe, and he would come to visit me often. He and Mondre' got along well, and Mondre''s girlfriend and daughter moved in. After a few weeks, I found out I was pregnant. To this day, I'm not sure if it was the hormones. Or the fact I stopped doing drugs had anything to do with it, but I became a nightmare to be around. My little brother put me out of his house.

Temporarily, I went back to live with Sharda. She had an studio apartment and was never home but often with one of her many men. When I found out I was pregnant, my first decision was to have an abortion. I shared this information with another close friend, Joie, and did not tell Sharda I was pregnant. I made an appointment with the clinic on the following Friday when I got paid and decided to go through with the procedure. Once again, I felt like I had made one of the worst decisions in my life by getting pregnant. Being a mama scared me to death, and I did not want to fail someone who had no choice but to depend on me.

The morning of my appointment, Joie drove me there. We

sat in the car for an hour. For some odd reason, I could not find it in myself to follow through with my original decision. I called Poe and told him I was pregnant and about my plan to have an abortion. He went crazy because he wanted to keep the baby. He told me all I had to do was sign over my rights, and I would not be responsible for anything for our child. I agreed. Joie and I left the clinic.

Within a week, Poe moved to Houston, and we got an apartment together. I worked two months before the doctors put me on bed rest. I had a high-risk pregnancy. I could not smoke or pop any pills. I was miserable. I did not know what was worse, being pregnant or being incarcerated. I stayed at home all day, mostly alone. Poe was admitted to the University of Houston and worked two jobs. All I did was read and write. I did not want to talk to anyone or be seen by anyone. The baby growing inside of me was the only person I had to talk to. So, I talked to him often and about everything. I told him I never expected to have kids, and he would be a Legend one day. That was the first time I felt him move inside of me. I said Legend again, and he moved again. That was the name I settled on. We had a bond from that moment. I became increasingly more comfortable as my pregnancy went along, especially when I felt him move. When I did sneak out of the house, people would ask me what I was having throughout my pregnancy, and I intuitively told them I was having a boy. I knew God would not punish me with a girl. I did not know how my family would react, but I was 27 years old and cared for myself. Of course, with the help of Poe. But my granny on mama's side was ecstatic and told me it is something every woman should experience.

I expected my mama to be excited and come around more, but that did not happen. We barely even talked. An elegant and well-established woman adopted me in Houston and took me under her wing. Poe's family was there throughout my pregnancy. His grandma lived with us during my last trimester. I enjoyed her being around though. She cooked twice a day, and the house was always clean.

On February 13, 2015, I went into labor and experienced some of the worst pain of my life. I never plan to do it again. I had gained 65 pounds and the biggest I had ever been. Within ten minutes of being at the hospital, the doctor ordered the nurses to prepare me for a Cesarean Section. The nurses shaved my pelvic area then put some shocking's on my feet. I tried not to be the stubborn, troubled patient, but my contractions felt like someone stabbing me in the stomach repeatedly. They were coming every minute.

The nurses moved me to the operating room. There were no decorations on the wall but a reclined hospital chair that was half-covered with a large blue sheet coming down from the ceiling, a small table with what looked like a metal bowl sitting on a scale, and a vanity sink. At first, I did not notice the substantial amount of blood next to my chair until I sat down. I asked the doctor what the blood was for, and he explained that since I had a high-risk pregnancy and, in my condition, I could lose a lot of blood and need a blood transfusion. My anxiety kicked in, and all I could think about was everything that could go wrong while I was in labor. I panicked even more when I noticed Poe was not in the room. He finally came in after he put on his blue outfit, mask, and hair cover.

Within minutes, Legend was here. He was crying when he came into the world. Poe got upset with the doctors and asked them what they did to him. The nurse asked him to calm down, but Legend continued crying, and Poe was getting angrier. Moments later after Poe and Legend calmed down, they handed me my son, and I held him for the first time. Mondre' and his girlfriend came to the hospital. Poe went back home to get his grandma because he had a college exam that afternoon, and he did not want me to be alone.

Face to Face with the Devil

After I had Legend, I continuously expected me and my mama's relationship to get better, but instead it got worse. Poe called her without my knowledge and said some horrible things to her. She changed her number, and I was unable to contact her. By this time Legend was 3 years old. I had continuously been reaching out to my mama through Mondre', my aunts, and grandparents, but all they would say was, "We are trying!"

I was a mother with a child, and my own mama would not speak with me. I did not understand why. Another year passed. Finally, Mondre' told me about the phone call she'd received from Poe. I hated Poe for it. I fell into a depression and became suicidal.

One Friday evening, I went to hang out with my friends. The girls and I decided to go to a local bar up the street. I usually did not consume alcoholic beverages, but I needed to relieve some stress, and at the end of the day, I just wanted to get fucked up! There were five of us in total, and the house special was $5 you call it. Their favorite drinks were Don Julio and Patron. They bought severa; rounds. After five shots or at least the last one I remembered, I did not feel drunk, so I continued drinking. I knew I had drunk a lot, but I did not feel it. I was a little tipsy, but I was okay.

We made it back to my friend's house around midnight. My friends asked me many times if I was okay to drive. I assured them I was and got into the car and headed up 288

North headed towards Interstate 45. I turned on some of my favorite tunes to keep me awake for the 30-minute drive. When I arrived home, Poe was asleep downstairs on the couch, so I got into bed. I woke up to darkness. I was chained and could not move for an extended period of time. Finally, able to break away from the chains, I ran through the darkness and fought like it was the end of my life. The entire time there was "this thing" that tormented and mocked me. I was terrified of it! I tried to escape, but there was nowhere for me to go, but I kept fighting!

Eventually, I got tired and didn't want to fight anymore. I almost gave up. Then I saw a small bright light. I rushed towards the light with all the strength I had. The closer I got, the more colorful it got. But it was not easy because now I was being taunted by many tiny "things." They held chains in their hands. They tried to wrap them around me. It was a horrifying experience. Reaching the light was bliss I'd never known existed.

When I came back to reality, everything was a blur. Ciara was there, lying on a mat on the floor next to my bed. I did not know why she was there and did not care. I was thirsty, and my mouth was dry. She took me to Pappasito's, but I did not eat much. I was exhausted and wanted to lay back down. We got our food to go, and she took me to her house. I went back to sleep. Later that night, I received a text from Sharda asking if I could still pick her up from the airport. I told her I was good and would be able to. Ciara dropped me off at home and I asked her why she was there. She told me I had blacked out, and they were afraid for me. I wanted to know who "they" were. She named three people. I asked her why they did not take me to the hospital, and she explained that I was coherent and talking to them, but all I would talk about was my mama and how she would not speak with me.

Confused, I went inside my two-story condominium, and I destroyed everything in sight. It looked like a hurricane-damaged it. I had broken all three of my 55-inch televisions, two laptops, and there were holes in the walls. The entire time I was fighting in my sleep, I was breaking stuff in my house. Poe said I was mad, and he could not control me. He did not know what to do so he called my friends for help. Luckily, Legend was out of town with his grandparents. Still, I was disgusted with myself and decided to give up drinking alcohol for good.

Patience is a Virtue

Another year went by, and my aunts promised me that they were still working on my mama. My aunt said she had given my mama my number so she could call and wish me a happy birthday. I was excited and waited for her phone call, but I never got it.

One day I was meeting with one of my mentors. He introduced me to one of his good friends, Barrett, the Chief Executive Officer of an Investment company. I gratefully accepted his card because I knew he would be the reason I would become rich one day. He invited me to lunch with him a few weeks later. The conversation did not go any way I expected it to go because he talked about Jesus and the bible the whole time. We even prayed four times during lunch. I was over it.

Barrett called me once a week and invited me to his church every chance he got. He texted and emailed me bible verses every day. I could not take it anymore. Eventually, I blocked him but the pain of my mama not speaking to me hurt like hell, and I was about to self-destruct again. Barrett stayed on my mind all day, so I decided to reach out to him. I took Barrett up on his offer and decided to join him at church. He was so excited because he was preaching that Sunday. I was happy for him, but I was in so much anguish and despair. I had not been to church for five years since I had gotten out of jail. I went to the altar and laid all my pain down.

At the end of church service, I had a missed call from an unknown number. I called the number back, but there was no answer. It went to auto voicemail. I went around the church, and everyone greeted me, and they said they would pray for me. During the ride home, the number called me back, but I had missed it again. I saw the missed call once I got home and decided to return the call once I got comfortable and ate. The number called me back once again as I finished eating. I answered. It was the last person I expected it to be. My mama!

She started the conversation by telling me she had a dream about me. In the dream, she said I had on a white gown, and I was fighting someone. We were rolling in the dirt, grass, and she could see blood everywhere, but she could not see the face of the person I was fighting. But I had defeated whoever it was. At the end of the dream, I stood to my feet, and my white gown was squeaky clean, and I did not have a stain on me.

Part 3

Peace at Last

While I was on my new spiritual journey, discipline became a priority. It was always something I lacked. I would go to bible study, Sunday school, and Church service regularly but the verse, "Be still and know that I am God," always stayed with me. One morning one of my church members texted me a bible verse, and it said, "Meditate on my word day and night."

I made it a goal to read the entire bible. Then, I asked God to give me the wisdom to translate his word. In doing that, I learned to focus my mind on God, who is all good things and the totality of all things in the universe. Every day I meditated, I learned to control my thoughts, and over time I noticed I was less angry but calmer. It prevented me from worrying. I spent hours meditating, and it became one of the most powerful lessons I learned in life.

I continued going to church 2 - 3 times a week. The women in the church began our own weekly service. I learned about the different names of God and his unchanging characteristics. I found myself falling in love with the unseen. I could feel a strong, powerful yet comforting spirit surrounding me. I enjoyed submitting to its almighty presence. Suddenly, relieved from all my burdens. Meditating on God became an addiction and a good one for the first time.

I became a better friend, a better daughter, a better sister, and most importantly, a better mother to my son. Still far from perfect and facing many troubles, but at least this time, I know I am not alone. I profoundly and gratefully understood that I could call upon my Lord and Savior in submission and prayer if I need anything. Meditation became an essential part of my day. I meditated and prayed first thing in the morning. Before I went to bed, I meditated and showed gratitude for the universe's mercy and grace throughout the day.

As I was healing and focusing on becoming my best self, I was forced to confront things I'd suppressed for years. Finally, I had faced most of my demons and began feeling more confident about myself and understanding the meaning of self-love.

The Pain I Overlooked

One night I was meditating in the most profound state of consciousness I'd ever experienced. I felt free. I was at peace and experiencing an abundance of bliss. I was in a state of mind I wished I could stay in forever. Suddenly, I saw my young self in an apartment complex that brought back dark, frightening memories. My heart instantly began beating faster, and I was awakened by an anxiety attack. It was 3:33 am. My shirt was soaked from sweat. I did not know what was happening because I had not had an anxiety attack in years. I laid there, afraid to go back to sleep but wondering what happened in the dream.

A few days went by before I allowed my mind to think about what occurred. Then, suddenly one night, the apartment complex popped up during meditation again. This time I tried to stay focused on it as long as I could. But the longer I tried to focus, the faster my heart would beat, and eventually, I would awake. I did not get any sleep for a month. I knew I was going to have to face whatever it was I had been running from. I'd persuaded myself the sooner, the better. So why not now? I have had so much progression, and this nightmare was haunting me, and I did not know why.

I took several deep breaths and allowed my mind to take me to that dark place. As I laid there, the nightmare slowly began to unravel. It was revealed to me that the man we thought was Mondre's daddy, OJ, sister's house. I was around six years old, and Mondre was 3 years old. OJ's sister would babysit me and Mondre on the weekend. I hated going to Pleasant Grove and would scream to the top of my lungs whenever my mama mentioned she was taking us over there. So I would call my granny to pick me up. Or even my dad. Anything so I would not have to go to that lady's house.

The dream continued. I saw the apartment's interior and OJ's sister and her three children. She had two daughters and a son. My heart started beating fast again, but I took deep breaths and maintained them until my heart rate went back to normal. I began focusing and realized how much OJ's sister and her daughters loved Mondre'. They spoiled him rotten and gave him anything he wanted. They would walk to the store to get him snack cakes, cookies, chips, and candy. Whatever he wanted. Sometimes he would share with me, but he did not most of the time because they told him not to. There were times when they cooked dinner, and everyone would eat except for me. They would force me to sit in the corner on the couch all weekend. I would watch everyone pass by. If someone spoke to me, it would make my day.

One weekend while I was there, I threw a fit because I was starving, and no one would give me anything to eat. While I was on my way to the bathroom, her teenage son whispered to me that he'd snuck me some food. I smiled at him with joy. He had asked his mama if we could go to the park across the street from their house. She agreed. I followed him to the park. He had stashed a cup of Chicken Ramen noodles into his baggy jeans. I smashed on the noodles as if they were my first and last meal ever.

The sun began going down, and the ice cream truck passed by. I got excited, and he asked me if I wanted anything. I told him I did. He agreed and said he would buy me anything I wanted if I went around the corner with him. So, I followed him to an abandoned apartment. He pulled down his pants and told me that he would give me whatever I wanted if I did what he told me to do. That was not the last time I was dropped off in Pleasant Grove. That was not the last time I was forced to do something for food.

During my journey, I faced my inner child and what happened to young, innocent me. I realized a lot of my anger and hate originated from that experience. Although this incident happened thirty years ago, I'd suppressed this pain, and I do not even remember his name. I forgave myself for blaming myself for so long and bringing so much injury to my adult self. I forgave him because I am sure he did not know any better. Finally, I forgave the people who left me behind because I felt someone should have been there to protect me. But through it all, I learned that it is not even about me at all, but every day is a gift. Everyone does not receive this gift. So graciously, take each day at a time. Let tomorrow worry about itself. Each moment is precious, and every breath is meant to be worshiped. It is a blessing just to tell you this story!

Valencia Lee began writing poetry when she was only eight years old to escape her harsh realties of her life. She has published over 10 books including young adult fiction, short stories, and faith & self help books and has assisted university professors, law enforcement officers, and community activists publish their books.

www.ingramcontent.com/pod-product-compliance
Lightning Source LLC
Chambersburg PA
CBHW071445300726
48976CB00004B/1445